Undermining the
Central Line

Ruth

RENDELL

&

Colin

WARD

Undermining
the
Central Line

Chatto & Windus
LONDON

Published in 1989 by
Chatto & Windus Ltd
30 Bedford Square
London WC1B 3SG

A CIP catalogue record for this book
is available from the British Library

ISBN 0 7011 3598 0

Photoset in Linotron Ehrhardt by
Rowland Phototypesetting Ltd
Bury St Edmunds, Suffolk
Printed in Great Britain by
St Edmundsbury Press Ltd
Bury St Edmunds, Suffolk

Contents

Sleepers Awake

UTOPIANS OF every kind have an unaccountable habit of waking up in the next century in order to describe the impact of history. Who cares about the details? It's the discoveries that matter.

We had lived in adjacent parishes, Kersey and Polstead in Suffolk, and had seen our villages change, for better but more often for worse. Arising with no symptoms of time-lag, we were wildly curious about what might have happened. The year was 2051, halfway through a new century.

Kersey is a dream village visually and has been called the most beautiful in Suffolk. It is a compact, tightly-built mediaeval town, once a centre of the wool trade, and its one big street leads down to a ford full of ducks and geese. In 1980 the youth club there was wound up because there were too few young people. 'It really is a dying village,' said the organiser, and the then county education officer described the village school as 'a rather dingy room with clapped-out furniture' – a clear indication, we thought, of the county's intention to close it, once the head teacher had reached retirement age.

It was a relief to find, seventy years later, that the village had not died. Only a little more ancient, the ancient houses were still there. The school was not only still open but had expanded. It had become a focus of activity by day and night. The new homes of the Kersey Housing Co-op, built on the higher land around this deep valley, explained why. Down by the riverside we pondered another long-term change. In the 1970s Kersey Mill and the Maltings had been derelict, the owner served with a notice by the council that unless he maintained the buildings they would be compulsorily purchased.

If they had done so we would have had yet another heritage museum on our hands. We were lucky that a purchaser set up a computer factory there and put a coat of paint on the old mill. In the twenty-first century we found the old mill actually working, not by a loving reconstruction of the ancient wooden waterwheel, but through new smooth-running stainless steel paddles channelling the River Brett to generate electricity for local needs. Making our way down towards Hadleigh, we found more such mill-races, gathering power from a series of tiny sources.

But we were bound for the next destination, Polstead, a sprawling, dispersed village with several different central areas – the pond, the pub, the river bridge, the church and the village hall. With the good luck that attends every visitor from another age, we fell in with an obliging guide. Something about her seemed familiar and we were not surprised to find that her great-grandmother had been a friend of ours from the 1980s. There was no need for tedious explanations. She accepted us readily as enquiring visitors, hungry for news of change.

One change that had not taken place was in the village shop, and we were relieved to see this community venture still thriving. We well remembered how it had been opened in 1982 when, the village having been without a shop for twenty years, a few people tried the experiment of starting their own, at first in a caravan, and later in purpose-built premises. When we saw it surviving into another century, we felt their faith and hard work had been rewarded. We had an even bigger surprise when we arrived at the school to find it not closed but enlarged, and thronged with fellow-citizens large and small, infants and teenagers.

We recalled the apparently fruitless struggle to keep the school alive, the fight against the authority of a Government document, a delegation to the Education Minister by our local MP, and we remembered how, in the 1990s, the County Education Department sold the school building as a private house for a large sum of money.

Our guide had to explain to us the huge turnaround in thinking that had recovered and extended Polstead School early in the twenty-first century to accord with a new view of education. And she was obliged to make still more explanations when she took us to the stop of the Box Valley Light Railway. As the railcar arrived from Boxford, down the line, she recalled to us how, in the nineteenth century, railways had become a universal form of transport. Even as early as 1847 the Hadleigh and Eastern Union Junction Railway Company's extension from the London–Ipswich–Norwich main line was serving passengers from our neighbourhood.

In 1932 it was closed for passengers and in 1965 for goods when the Beeching Axe closed down hundreds of branch lines. But at the beginning of the century where we now found ourselves a new trend had arisen – the Democratic Railway Movement, demanding that the advantages of rail travel should be available to all. Slowly the branch lines revived, taking advantage of new technologies. As our train passed through the newly subdivided and intensive smallholdings on the beautiful route from Polstead, we realised what a revolution in thinking had taken place. We came to the restored Hadleigh Station through the nature reserve created out of the old line from Hadleigh that was once called the Railway Walk.

But the pleasure we took in the school, the shop and the branch line distracted us from the most important lesson we should have learned from our guided tour. Dazzled by new technologies, we had very nearly missed the intense discussions in progress that Sunday morning in the village hall, the

4

church, the 'Shoulder of Mutton' and 'Cock' taverns, and on the green itself.

The citizens of Polstead were making key decisions on dozens of issues. For instance, they were deciding on the level of income on which they should tax themselves. Familiar with the principle of tithing (i.e. that everyone should devote one tenth of his or her income to public purposes), they were discussing the disposition of this revenue. They debated the extent of relief from tax citizens could earn by working on community projects and disputed the amounts to be paid over to the Anglian Regional Council in Norwich and to the Federal Council, this latter situated, we learned, not in London but Milton Keynes.

We listened to their argument and gradually understood that the content of political debate in Polstead was not about Right and Left but about localism, regionalism and centralism, and their place in people's lives. Since in our day these things were seldom if ever discussed, we were at first bewildered, then intensely interested.

'Why don't you come along to my WEA class in the pub this afternoon?' she said. 'I'm just reaching the last thirty years.' It was a lecture on social history. We listened carefully as she explained the politics of the twentieth century to the citizens of the twenty-first. Our own times were presented in terms of the struggles between imperialism and

5

nationalism, then between Right and Left, private profit or public enterprise. 'By the end of the century,' she said, 'different kinds of polarities arose: between governments and people or between national and local.'

Older members of the group nodded in agreement as she described the bitter battles of the early years of the twenty-first century, the way in which irresistible demands for independence in Scotland and Wales inevitably led to the campaign for autonomy in the English regions. We sensed indignation in the air when the class came to discuss the Treasury Riots of 2010. 'Why were they called that?' someone asked. 'Because the Treasury was the name of the central government's department which monopolised the people's treasure. It alone could gather revenue and this was the last power the government was willing to give up.'

The members of the class found this an incomprehensible situation and a patient explanation had to be given that in Britain local councils had been a creation of central government rather than the other way around. Their powers had been more and more constrained by successive governments all through the twentieth century – until, as she put it, the worm turned.

It was familiar history to us. We were impatient to learn what happened next, but the sheer weight of new impressions we had gathered that day, or the impact of Polstead ale, had made us drowsy. In our corner of the bar we fell asleep. And like all Utopian dreamers, we woke up in the old world, in our case in the Polstead and Kersey of 1989, and in, of course, the political climate of that year.

Locally, we were faced with issues such as the decline of public transport, the imminent closure of the village school, and the fact that when its pupils became adults they would be unable to rent or buy a home in their own village.

Armed with our glimpse of the future, we concluded that one of the big issues of the last decade of our own century was that local people had no control over most of the basic everyday aspects of their own lives. This applied as much to towns, cities and suburbs as to our villages where these issues could be reduced to a comprehensible neighbourhood scale.

Not that we are suggesting it was ever very different. The past of our cosy patch of Suffolk was far worse. Looking back to 1830, historians remark that, 'It does not take much imagination to picture the situation of famished dependence of the sixty per cent of *all* inhabitants of Hitcham or Polstead, or of almost the entire population of Wattisham and Whatfield . . . who were paupers.' The past was immeasurably more hopeless. But our concern must be with the future.

7

Why did we both have premonitions of a decentralised future for the villages where we happen to live? We must have absorbed something from the history of another European country which neither of us knows much about nor cares much about, though we each chance to have family connections there. Comparing notes, we found that it was Switzerland which had been our common mentor. In 1830 its inhabitants were as poor as their English counterparts. By 1990 they, *per capita*, were the richest people in Europe.

Success is derided and it is true that the great Swiss writers of our time, such as Max Frisch or Friedrich Dürrenmatt, endlessly attack the foundations of the society which produced them. This is normal and natural but not relevant to the Swiss experience, which overturns all our British assumptions about the role of central government and the scope of local intervention.

Lessons from Switzerland

IN MARCH 1989 a series of performances of Schiller's play *William Tell* were given at the Crucible Theatre in Sheffield. The hero enjoys the same place in Swiss mythology as Robin Hood does in English. The play shows him as the simple local hero who saw how the Austrian Empire had insidiously taken over Swiss self-government, while the Swiss, intent on staying alive, scarcely noticed what was happening.

When Verdi's *Nabucco* was first performed at La Scala in 1842 the audience, recognising a parallel between the drama before them and their own situation, rose to their feet and cheered. The theme of the opera, the hope of liberty and self-government, identified Verdi for the first time with his country's political aspirations. It would have been marvellous to report that the Crucible audiences followed the Milan example. Sheffield's councillors, who cannot conceivably be associated with any aspect of the governmental demonology of the 'loony Left', have tried to cope with the catastrophic decline of local industry and have found at every step that their attempts are *ultra vires*, or in other words, that they are stepping beyond their legal powers. This could not possibly happen in, say, France, West Germany, Italy or the United States. We are inevitably led back to William Tell country. The Swiss, in a land with hardly any natural resources, were obliged for centuries to establish their version of local autonomy and to make a living for themselves. Gradually, across linguistic, ethnic and cultural divisions, they evolved a system of administration so complex yet so remarkably democratic that it is astounding it has not been emulated everywhere else. Our dream of the future of our own parishes must have been influenced by Herbert Luethy's account of the way it works:

> Every Sunday, the inhabitants of scores of communes go to the polling booths to elect their civil servants, ratify such and such an item of expenditure, or decide whether a road or a school should be built; after settling the business of the commune, they deal with cantonal elections and voting on cantonal issues; lastly, like surface waves sweeping at rarer intervals across water that is constantly stirring in its depths, come the decisions on federal issues. In some cantons, the sovereign people still meet in Rousseau-like fashion to discuss questions of common interest. It may be thought that this ancient form of assembly is

no more than a pious tradition with a certain value as a tourist attraction. If so, it is worth looking at the results of local democracy.

The point that Luethy goes on to make explains why we would be foolish to ignore the Swiss experience.

The simplest example is the Swiss railway system, which is the densest network in the world . . . It has been made to serve the needs of the smallest localities and most remote valleys, not as a paying proposition but because such was the will of the people . . . The railway map is the easiest to read at a glance, but let us now superimpose on it another showing economic activity and the movement of population. The distribution of industrial activity all over Switzerland, even in the outlying areas, and the existence in small country towns of businesses with international connections, account for the strength and stability of the social structure of the country and prevented those horrible nineteenth-century concentrations of industry, with their slums and rootless proletariat.

The Chief Officer of a Welsh county council, Ioan Bowen Rees, carefully identified the lessons of Switzerland for British local government. He was commenting on the background to government commissions on the future of local government in the sixties and seventies.

The commissions and committees and the evidence submitted to them were dominated by two issues: uniformity and size. Whether a two-tier or a unitary system was advocated, it was assumed that any service needed a vast population in order to be efficient and economical. Government departments themselves were in no doubt. 'Almost unanimously, the Ministries had pleaded for thirty to forty first-tier or all-purpose authorities in England. Their evidence abounds with such phrases as "below somewhere around the 200,000 mark we do begin to run into difficulties," and "half a million is a good round figure".'

The Royal Commission chased the will o' the wisp of size as did the legislation that subsequently established the present subdivisions of English local government. One of its members, the late Derek Senior, wrote a minority report which today is more in demand than the main document. He dismissed the mountain of research that the Commission had drawn upon with the comment that 'the one thing these researches have put beyond doubt is that no positive correlation whatever between population, size and performance can be statistically established even in the present local government system.'

Mr Bowen Rees was outraged at the way the

central government in Britain invariably put the demands of administrators and professional providers of services before the needs of the local community. Similarly, Professor Ivor Gowan drew attention to the paradox that, 'Here we are thinking of population ranges of between 250,000 and 1,000,000 for our unitary authorities. In most other countries, even in the developed world, most of the population lives in "municipalities" or "communes" with a population of less than 2,000.'

But of all nations, the one which most startlingly contradicts British assumptions is Switzerland. As the Swiss see no need for uniformity, and would have no means of centrally enforcing it, the population of a commune can range from fifty to 500,000. The services provided vary accordingly. At one end of the scale a commune provides education, supports the poor, maintains minor roads, provides water and sewers, cares for the environment, and is the legislative as well as the executive authority for building standards and planning. At the other, a group of tiny communes combine to provide a primary school. And at their disposal the communes have almost the whole range of taxes open to a state.

There may be readers who will respond to this account of Swiss democracy with a sneer at its trifling parochialism. But this must depend on the standards by which it is judged. Let Mr Bowen

Rees speak here with some observations he made years before the Thatcher government's assault on British local government in the name of cost-effectiveness:

> To many Englishmen today the object of local government is to provide efficient services, to give the ratepayer his money's worth. At a recent international conference on Amalgamation and Co-operation, the Chief Whip of the Greater London Council said that the only yardstick that could be used was 'the finest service at the cheapest possible price', whereupon a NALGO representative interposed that 'as local government was big business, the methods of big business should be employed'. In Switzerland the principal object of local government is still to enable a locality to retain as much freedom as possible. How else can one explain the existence of a strong movement, independent of the state, to encourage wealthy lowland communes to help poor Alpine communes to provide better amenities without having to succumb to bureaucracy and lose their identity?

Switzerland, he concludes, is a welfare society rather than a welfare state, and its communities behave responsibly because *they* and no central directing authority *are* responsible.

Could we imagine the Switzerisation of Britain? Ioan Bowen Rees does not hesitate to apply the lessons he learned to his native Wales, but ruefully reflects that 'one must concede that it would be unwise to try to introduce a system as highly decentralised and democratic as that of the Swiss into the United Kingdom in the course of a few years'; and Jonathan Steinberg, in *Why Switzerland?*, flatly declares, 'I am not so foolish as to set one society up to be imitated by another. The reasons why the Swiss trust the people and the British do not go deep into the very different histories of the two societies.'

But the irony is that the British *do* think Swiss. Nothing arouses more genuine passion than campaigns to Save Our School or Keep Our Railway Open. Hence the unending popularity of those Ealing comedies: *Passport to Pimlico* and *The Titfield Thunderbolt*. Where we have failed is in translating these universal sentiments into political action. We have surrendered localist feelings to professional politicians and to central government's civil servants and professional advisers.

The Attrition of the Local

'WELL,' SAID HE, 'let us take one of our units of management, a commune, or a ward, or a parish . . . In such a district, as you would call it, some neighbours think that something ought to be done or undone: a new town hall built; a clearance of inconvenient houses; or say a stone bridge substituted for some ugly old iron one – there you have undoing and doing in one. Well, at the next ordinary meeting of the neighbours, or Mote, as we call it, according to the ancient tongue of the times before bureaucracy, a neighbour proposes the changes and of course, if everybody agrees, there is an end of discussion, except about details . . . But supposing the affair proposed and seconded, if a few of the neighbours disagree to it, if they think that the beastly iron bridge will serve a little longer and they don't want to be bothered with building a new one just then, they don't count the heads that time, but put off the formal discussion to the next Mote; and meantime arguments pro and con are flying about, and some get printed, so that everybody knows what is going on; and when the Mote comes together again there is a regular discussion and at last a vote by show of hands.

'If the division is a close one, the question is again put off for further discussion; if the division is a wide one, the minority are asked if they will yield to the more general opinion, which they often, nay, most commonly, do. If they refuse, the question is debated a third time when, if the minority has not perceptibly grown, they always give way; though I believe there is some half-forgotten rule by which they might still carry it on further; but I say, what always happens is that they are convinced, not perhaps that their view is the wrong one, but they cannot force the community to adopt it.'

'Very good,' said I, 'but what happens if the divisions are still narrow?'

Said he, 'As a matter of principle and according to the rule of such cases, the question must then lapse; and the majority, if so narrow, has to submit to sitting down under the *status quo*. But I must tell you that in point of fact the minority very seldom enforces this rule, but generally yields in a friendly manner.'

'But do you know,' said I, 'that there is something in all this very like democracy; and

I thought that democracy was considered to be in a moribund condition many many years ago.'

Thus William Morris writing in 1890 at the beginning of what has been called the Golden Age of local government in Britain. Before 1888 something like chaos prevailed with ancient corporations unreformed, health boards, improvement commissioners, boards of guardians and boards of trustees, the Church and numerous charitable offices struggling for ascendancy. The two Local Government Acts of 1888 and 1894 between them created county councils, county borough councils, urban district and rural district councils. Parishes were revived by the creation of parish councils and that most lowly (but perhaps most purely Utopian) arm of local government, the parish meeting.

Local government as we know it was completed as a system in 1899 when the London County Council was formed and twenty-eight metropolitan boroughs established for what at that time was the world's most populous city. Local authorities had a constitutional basis with rational principles and open democracy as their foundation, a system very like Morris's deceptively unsophisticated theory.

The state was happy to transfer many of its increasing responsibilities from central government. Among other functions local authorities assumed were responsibility for education when the old School Boards were abolished in 1902 and for welfare after the dissolution of the Boards of Guardians. The former administrative functions of the Justices of the Peace became theirs: rating, licensing, highways, weights and measures and police. The provision of housing became a function of metropolitan, urban and district councils much earlier than is generally known. One million council houses were built in this country between 1919 and 1939. Local authorities participated in a national network of labour exchanges and had powers to finance the voluntary emigration of the chronically unemployed.

This 'Golden Age' peaked between the two World Wars and by the mid-1930s was in retreat, a decline which it does not take much political acumen or wise hindsight to see as the consequence of an eroding policy of centralisation.

But are we actually proud of the decay of local administration? You have only to visit the town halls of Birmingham, Manchester or Leeds, or the city chambers in Glasgow, to see how much magnificence the city fathers were willing to invest in glorifying their towns, long before the parliamentary legislation that justified their existence.

They were charged with the great task of looking after local interests and they set about discharging their responsibilities with enormous energy, regardless of political allegiances. From the 1870s onwards Joseph Chamberlain preached the municipal gospel in Birmingham, declaring that, 'Local government is near the people, local government will bring you into contact with the masses. By its means you will be able to increase their comforts, to secure their health, to multiply the luxuries which they may enjoy in common, to carry out a vast co-operative system for mutual aid and support, to lessen the inequalities of our social system and to raise the standard of all classes in the community.'

Any who imagine that the current onslaught by central government on the activities of city councils is the result of recent excesses of municipalisation by Labour authorities should reflect on an account of Glasgow in 1903, written before the Labour Party was formed. An observer wrote that a resident

may live in a municipal house; he may walk along the municipal street, or ride in the municipal tramcar and watch the municipal dustcart collecting the refuse which is used to fertilise the municipal farm. Then he may turn to the municipal market, buy a steak from an animal killed in the municipal slaughterhouse, and cook it by the municipal gas stove. For his recreation he can choose amongst municipal libraries, municipal art galleries and municipal music in municipal parks. Should he fall ill, he can ring up his doctor on the municipal telephone, or he may be taken to the municipal hospital in the municipal ambulance by a municipal policeman. Should he be so unfortunate as to get on fire, he will be put out by a municipal fireman, using municipal water; after which he will, perhaps, forgo the enjoyment of a municipal bath, though he may find it necessary to get a new suit in the municipal old clothes market.

The most important aspect of this list is not the reflection that it may have imposed a great burden on the ratepayers, but the opposite. Many of these functions were income-generating, or were trading operations which reduced that burden. In 1987 Don Simpson, who is the borough housing officer for Rochdale Metropolitan Borough Council in Lancashire, listed the functions of Rochdale Borough in 1906, putting asterisks against those which were major trading concerns. His list was:

Police
Gas manufacture and distribution*
Water supply and drainage*
Electricity generation and distribution*
Highways
Libraries/art gallery/museum/parks
Tramways*
Education

He comments that today 'council housing is the *only* large-scale trading operation which the council runs. House renting is, of course, a public service as well as a business, but it *is* a business.' He went on to conclude that 'the activities of the council have changed so much since 1906 that I infer that it is possible to be a supporter of a strong and democratic system of local government *without* committing oneself to any particular or fixed list of municipal functions. The case for the council, and for local democracy, does not collapse just because the council is no longer a large-scale landlord.' But on this point Mr Simpson has a vital reservation. His view is that the Thatcher government 'seems intent on poisoning its own water by not coming up with any coherent plan or process for alternative *social* – as opposed to commercial – ownership of estates'.

We *do* have an alternative, but we must first pursue the implications of the *de-localisation* of everything. In the 1980s central governments, relying for their authority on a statistical minority of voters, and even in the case of unimportant appendages to their realm like Scotland, on a minority of Members of Parliament, decided to sell in the private market a series of natural monopolies, including transport and services, and to toy with the idea of privatising the hospital service.

The fact that these measures are possible arises

directly from the centralising activities of earlier governments. For example, the one thing most people know about the city of Hull is that the telephones belong to the city council and that the call boxes are white, not red. Eighty years ago a Liberal government brought the entire telephone system under the control of the General Post Office. Hull declined to conform. When the system was sold off in the 1980s the irony was that Hull was the only place where telephones remained, and still remain, in public ownership. Local calls stay cheaper, and as an extra twist of irony it is one of the few places where the ordinary domestic consumer really has a choice for long-distance calls between the allegedly free choice of Telecom and Mercury.

In 1945 the incoming Labour government was not prepared to let any local council opt out of any centralised system. Clement Attlee had warned, back in the 1930s, that a Labour government would employ commissioners who would be 'sent down into a locality to see that the will of the central government is obeyed and its plans implemented'.

The plans were implemented. A host of local services like hospitals, with their huge range of origins as municipal, voluntary, charitable or Poor Law institutions, or like gas and electricity with an equally varied range of local initiatives behind them, were taken over by central bodies and removed from local control. In the succeeding decades cottage hospitals were closed in favour of vast all-purpose institutions, as were local generating undertakings. Small Public Assistance Committees became first the National Assistance Board and later The Supplementary Benefits Commission. Transport Acts transferred responsibility for roads and road transport, rivers, canals and harbours, to various central authorities.

Not only did local councils lose their responsibilities to central government but also within their own hierarchy. In 1944 district councils lost to county councils their function of providing elementary education, in 1946 they lost their health and police functions and a year later their responsibility for fire services and planning. In the case of the police, centralisation has intensified in that many forces are no longer run by one county authority. Joint committees of neighbouring county councils administer them – a far cry from the American system where every city, and in numerous cases the small township, provides its own police force.

Problems of finance have far-reaching effects in every area of life and loss of financial independence contributed here. As well as by the rates local authorities received income by way of rents, sales, service charges, fines and legacies. From the beginning, in the nineteenth century, there have been grants from central government and during the past

24

forty years this percentage of revenue has grown substantially. We will not be surprised to find that this has led to a much greater control and influence on the part of central government, not to mention powers of persuasion in local affairs.

The British political system has given our current rulers an absolute right to sell off services in the private market. But if we ask you, Reader, whose fault this is, you will have to agree that it is the fault of all of us, and our parents, in taking for granted that central government knows best.

Who Rules the Schools?

DEMOCRACY, according to the OED, is government by the people, and secondarily, *that form of government in which the sovereign power resides in the people, and is exercised either directly by them or by officers elected by them.* Collins Cobuild, among its definitions, gives: *A system of running organisations, businesses, groups etc, in which each member is entitled to vote and participate in management decisions.*

There is a difference here which, when examined, may seem to verge upon the sinister. The Collins dictionary, after all, is far more recent, more 'modern'. The word *entitled* strikes us with its implications of a right that may be no more than a right, a mere empty exercise which may never succeed in affecting decision or changing inexorability. Such a definition can only ring with an awful truth in the ears of the people of Polstead who, believing that sovereign power resided in them as citizens of a democracy, found the truth to be quite otherwise.

Far from the ideal future outlined in our Utopian dream, Polstead School will close in 1990 and its pupils will be transferred to the neighbouring village of Stoke-by-Nayland. This will be in direct opposition to the will of almost everyone living in

Polstead and certainly of those whose children attend the school, surely a group whose opinion should be of overriding significance.

Many of them (and their parents and forebears) attended the school themselves. An easy and happy relationship has existed between teachers and parents, the latter bringing their children to school and collecting them at the end of the day, often a matter of not much more than walking across the road. Parents have attended courses organised by West Suffolk Education Centre and participate in teaching. The Friends of Polstead School, by their fund-raising events, have provided equipment for physical education, television, video and computer equipment, and books. The quality of education at the school is outstanding. Levels of literacy and numeracy are exceptionally good and the number of children requiring remedial attention is low. Parents have found that their children going on to Middle School have had to wait for children from elsewhere to catch up with them.

It is in a lovely place. The building is Victorian red brick situated in a quiet lane near the village centre and with a delightful view of meadows and woodland. The roll – from a low point of twenty-two in 1979, following transition to a three-tier system in West Suffolk – has grown to reach fifty each summer during the past three years. Experienced primary school teachers suggest that forty to fifty pupils in a school catering for five- to nine-year-olds is the ideal size.

When the school goes the part it plays in the community life of the village will be lost. An end will come to the progression of community involvement from the mother and toddler group to the play-group and primary school, leading on to member-ship of the youth club (a facility lacking in other villages whose young people come to Polstead for this), and then to other forms of commitment to the life of the village, such as the community shop in which youngsters already help.

Three hundred thousand pounds is to be spent on rebuilding the Stoke-by-Nayland School. For a fraction of that the existing buildings at Polstead could be extended to cater for a three-teacher school to modern standards. It is a mile to Stoke-by-Nayland, for some children much further, and some parents have already been made nervous by the speed at which traffic dashes along these narrow winding lanes. Bussing is inevitable but the journey each way on an unsupervised bus, in the company of older children, will disrupt the day, particularly for the youngest. For some the cost will be difficult to manage. In whatever way the cost is met it will be an extra charge to the community.

The school's Support Committee have called it a 'centre of excellence'. The traditional strengths of the smaller village school, including the pupils' feeling of belonging within the community, are present. Kenneth Baker, Secretary of State for Education, himself said (before the last general election) that such schools 'provide the cement for the community', and pledged the Conservative Party to support small village schools. The present Government has much to say about the duty of their seniors to give moral leads to young people. Closure of this school, on the other hand, will weaken such influences on Polstead's children in their formative years. It is perhaps nearer the mark to suggest that this Government knows very well what one of the effects of its small school closure policy will be – that of inducing a greater proportion of parents to opt for private education.

For, ironically, our village has provided in the past an institution that had all the advantages and charms of a private school and none of its draw-backs. Where else but in the English village has it been possible for children to go no more than a few hundred yards to school, find themselves when there among their peers and neighbours, look out on the same view they see from home, be part of a small class and receive the maximum individual attention, know that in many cases mother and father and older siblings attended here before them, sitting perhaps at these same desks? And all this, if we discount the education burden, in any case obligatory, on ratepayers, was to be had for free.

In two years' time it will all be in the past. Without a miracle, there will be no school for us to visit in that twenty-first-century Utopia. Perhaps schooling will no longer be compulsory, perhaps that ideal of all creators of Utopias will have come to pass, and people will pick up their education where and when they need it. But if that is so, for good or ill, it will not be by the will of the people in Polstead now. The wish of an overwhelming majority was for the school to remain open. They 'share a real sense of outrage', said the School Support Committee, 'at its proposed destruction and replacement at greatly increased cost . . . Is it really sensible when the school is doing so well to spend so much more on sending small children down the dangerous lane to Stoke-by-Nayland, to larger classes and a school that is going to have to start from scratch, when money is so desperately needed elsewhere in Suffolk schools?

'Please think carefully. The quality of many lives rests on your judgement.'

Whether the Secretary of State, to whom this appeal was directed, did think carefully we shall never know. Certain it is that the plea was refused. 'We, the undersigned,' it begins, '*being local government electors in the area concerned* (our italics) hereby register our objection in the strongest possible terms.' The Suffolk County Council's policy to revive the closure proposal they called 'arbitrary, unreasonable and vindictive'.

All to no avail. The conclusion that the people of Polstead had no control whatsoever over this important aspect of their lives is impossible to avoid. It would be hard to name a function of the community more important than education, but in this democracy (not so-termed by us but reiteratively by the Prime Minister) those most directly and personally concerned with it, those *local government electors in the area concerned*, were unable by their concerted and 'strongest possible' efforts to turn the rolling tide of dominance by central government. They were powerless. If they believed that sovereign power resided in them, they were deluded.

◇

There is a rather curious footnote to the sorry business of school closures.

Apathy and seeming indifference in local politics are what we all become accustomed to. Much of it, we would suggest, is due to experience of the ineffectiveness of protest. Electors in another part of Suffolk have recently demonstrated two points: one that, with energy and determination, they have the power to sway events, the other that they will not sit down resignedly under the flagrant disregard of local wishes.

Sir Macdonald Miller, the Chairman of Suffolk County Council, as Chairman of the Suffolk Education Committee, presided over the decision to close Reydon High School. As a result he has lost his seat and, inevitably, his chairmanship. Southwold Conservative Association refused to readopt him as their candidate in the May 1989 County Council elections.

His own comment is perhaps the best example of what we (and Suffolk electorates) find so inimical to just and concerned local government. Of the Southwold Conservatives he said,

'They were at variance with central government policy – the Secretary of State confirmed the proposals.'

Sir Macdonald's successor, the official Conservative candidate, was opposed only by an Independent, Graham Langley. He made a name for himself as leader of the unsuccessful fight against the closure of Reydon High School.

In the May election he won the seat.

Will they get a House?

NICKY AND STEPHEN (not their real names) are a couple in their early twenties who each come from old, established Polstead families. Nicky's ancestors are listed as farmers among the principal inhabitants in that great gazetteer and history of 1844, *White's Suffolk*. We find Stephen's great-great-grandfather in the same directory named as a wheelwright. What present-day Polstead householder, having purchased a two hundred thousand pound home in the village environs, could boast such a pedigree?

Two years ago they began their married life in the small third bedroom of Nicky's parents' council house. Although their names were on Babergh District Council's housing list, no accommodation had been offered them and they hoped to buy a home of their own. The cottage in a village two miles away which was within their means if they both continued to work and took out a large mortgage, was on the market at thirty thousand pounds. It had a kitchen but no bathroom, running water and electricity, two rooms up and two down. Negotiations to buy it had begun when an estate agent stepped in and advised the vendor to withdraw the house from sale and re-offer it at fifty thousand.

This was far more than they could afford. All they could do was continue as they were, in the local authority accommodation already shared with Nicky's parents, her young sister and grown-up brother. Eventually, Babergh offered them a flat but in Lavenham, some seven miles away.

Britain has been called a property-owning democracy. As things are, to own property is no longer possible for a large section of the population, namely young rural workers. In order to buy a house or flat they must leave the community in which they were born and brought up and where in many cases their parents and ancestors were born and seek something within their means among the terraces and ribbon development surrounding the large country towns. Their own locality is closed to them. Property there is available only to commuting yuppies, wealthy professionals or retired people with pricey London houses to sell.

With the number of council houses dwindling as local authorities are empowered, indeed encouraged, to sell to sitting tenants, fewer and fewer must inevitably be available for rent. 'Very poor countries,' says Boleat in *National Housing Finance Systems*, 'tend to have very high levels of owner-occupation,' a comment into which it would be pessimistic to read too much sinister significance. Even owner-occupiers who can command high

34

prices for the homes they have for sale baulk at the prices asked for houses in our villages, an hour by train from London if you don't mind adding on half an hour in a car at one end and the same in a tube at the other. A terraced cottage costs eighty thousand pounds, a detached house three times that. Only a limited amount of land is available for building and when someone's orchard is permitted to be sold for 'infilling', a single five-bedroom ranch beyond the means of all but the rich will be built on it.

For Nicky and Stephen and their friends, those people who went to Polstead school in its heyday, there is nothing. The will of the people of Polstead and all those communities which make up the District of Babergh would certainly be that Nicky and Stephen should be offered a house within their means in their native village. But it is not in human nature to expect someone with property to sell, the product of a lifetime's mortgage repayments, to ask a lower than currently acceptable market price from motives of altruism. If the local authority builds more houses it must also offer them for sale to its tenants who again – and who would venture to criticise actions we would all in like circumstances succumb to? – will re-sell to private buyers at twice what they themselves paid.

Peter – another pseudonym – is the son of a Polstead farmer. His family once owned pieces of land in all corners of our scattered tripartite village. Next year he is getting married and he wants to build a house on his father's farm. The house he has in mind would not be large or obtrusive, a mansion in the middle of a meadow, but a bungalow set among other buildings which include his parents' home and the ancient original farmhouse.

Peter works for his father. He means to work on the land all his life and in the fulness of time take over the farm. When he applied to Babergh District Council for planning permission he made a point of calling on villagers to ask for their support. He particularly appealed to members of the parish council. Now parish councils in Britain, under the present system, have no planning powers. Their powers in general are restricted, having reference chiefly to the spending of a small budget derived from the district authority on small village projects. In theory, they exert influence on the higher authority but in practice their recommendations are mostly over-ridden, a far cry from a Utopian – or Swiss – commune.

'I want to live in Polstead all my life,' Peter said simply. 'I was born here. This is my place and I'd like to stay here always.' A house of this kind, built on land already belonging to his father, would be what Peter and his future wife could afford. Property coming up for sale in and around the village is far beyond their means. With almost unanimous village support behind him and the united support of the parish council, Peter thought he had a good chance. In spite of the land in question being outside the conservation area, and in spite of the recommendation and so-called 'influence' of the parish council, his application was turned down.

A laudable desire on the part of Babergh to maintain Polstead's rural character? A determination to restrict house-building in the vicinity of an Area of Outstanding Natural Beauty? Perhaps. But such sensitivity did not prevent permission being granted for a caravan park or for a pair of garages on a rustic site in historic sequestered Marten's Lane. More than that, it was the will of Polsteadians, with scarcely a dissenting voice, that Peter should have his house of the kind he wanted and where he wanted it. For all the good they did, they might have remained silent.

The chances of Peter acquiring a council house in Polstead are very slight, much reduced now that available houses are increasingly sold to their occupiers. Of course he might be offered accommodation in some other part of the Babergh District – a vast area which extends from the seacoast in its eastern extremity to Hitcham in the north and Somerton in the west – but it is in Polstead that he works.

Today the ideological whims of a government that most people did not vote for affect every attempt to provide 'affordable' housing for the new generation of rural dwellers. Traditionally, the home of rural workers was, by ordinary standards, mean and squalid and was frequently 'a tied cottage'. The mid-twentieth century saw a transformation of rural life for the better and council housing was part of this transformation.

But by the 1970s there was widespread disillusionment with local authority housing because of the collapse of effective management and maintenance, grotesquely paternalistic attitudes towards tenants, and inappropriate design. Some advocated that local authorities should be enablers rather than providers and that the one solution was in transferring estates to tenant co-operatives. The incoming Conservative government of 1979 adopted first its Right to Buy policy and, more recently, the policy mendaciously called Tenants' Choice which is really about Landlords' Choice.

It is not for owner-occupiers to criticise those who have exercised the right to buy. If tenants who have paid rents for an adult lifetime realised the way in which the Housing Revenue Account was manipulated against them, they would clamour to take advantage of this right. What we need to stress is how the government, in pursuing its antipathy towards the housing regime in certain cities, has denied *all* local authorities in Britain the opportunity to fulfil their statutory duty of housing the homeless, and of housing the next generation.

Regardless of local circumstances, this campaign has been followed with relentless central attention to detail, so that the moment any local body, whether statutory or voluntary, discovers a way of coping, central government finds a new obstacle. For example:

1. Local authorities aimed to devote revenues from the Right to Buy to provide further housing. Central government froze all but a tiny proportion of this.

2. Under Section 52 of the Town and Country Planning Act, 1971, a planning authority can enter into a voluntary agreement with an applicant, which can be used to secure provision of low-cost, low-rent housing. When the Lake District Special Planning Board tried to use Section 52 agreements to provide housing for local needs, as opposed to holiday or retirement homes, the Department of the Environment ruled against it.

3. Local authorities and housing associations sought to provide 'shared ownership' or 'shared equity' schemes, where the occupier has a right to increase his or her share of the property. Central government ruled that there is what the jargon calls a 'Right to Staircase', meaning that once full ownership is achieved, this housing can be sold in the private market. As Angela Sydenham says, 'It

is like trying to fill a leaky bucket – as soon as new low-cost homes are being added to the stock, others are being taken into the open market for private gain.'

4. By the 1980s a huge part of the cost of housing is the value of the land it is built on. Local authorities may own land acquired decades before but are forbidden to release it at a price below the District Valuer's assessment of its current speculative market valuation. If they did so, individual councillors could face prosecution and distraint procedures to recover the money 'lost'.

A grotesque accumulation of power in central government has prevented our local authorities in unimportant villages from doing anything effective about housing. Interested parties must look to alternatives. We would advise them to explore, in the absence of a flourishing local government housing policy, the potentialities both of housing co-operatives and self-build housing associations.

Since the Norfolk Rural Community Council was born in 1986, there have been thirty-seven more such bodies formed. They are a long way from the powerful and almost autonomous units of regional government we have in mind. Their members are, after all, amateurs and volunteers. But their very existence indicates a need for other

40

revised forms of local government and for an alternative to the weakened system as we know it. Among the concerns of ACRE – the Association of Community Councils in Rural England – are the shortage of affordable housing and the threatened loss of sub-post-offices. In 1988 the issue of affordable housing came to dominate all else and almost all Rural Community Councils have begun taking steps to ease the plight of those caught between rising prices in the private market and a diminishing stock of council housing. Rural housing associations are being formed and support given to existing urban housing associations. RCCs can play an entrepreneurial role involving the private sector. The housing associations they have created can build houses for rent exclusively. They can offer mixed-tenure schemes. All these aspects of housing can cause feelings to run high and must therefore be sensitively handled, which is where 'village appraisals' come in.

To date 250 English villages have been studied in this way – studies by local people, of the views of local people, for the benefit of local people. The strength of these studies lies in their synthesis of the views of the whole community, not just those of an articulate and 'socially-conscious' few. From our point of view, the new RCCs approach our regional government requirements in the nature of their membership which is of a local kind, drawn from voluntary and statutory bodies in the county itself.

Policies of central government affect them minimally. They are concerned almost entirely with the needs of the people within their scope – with Nicky and Stephen and Peter.

It Matters Everywhere

WE MAKE NO apology for our parochialism.
We have discussed two key issues, schooling and
housing, in relation to one village in prosperous
East Anglia, firstly because these issues are on our
doorstep and secondly to show that genuine local
democracy does not exist. The machinery of the
centralised state ensures that Polstead cannot run
its own affairs. Nor can our District Council, nor
can our County Council, both being controlled by
the political party that was elected to Westminster
with much rhetoric about 'rolling back the frontiers
of the state'.

The trend we can see in the country is glaringly
obvious in the cities. Urban Development Corporations, Urban Development Grants, City Action
Teams, Task Forces and Enterprise Zones, all
these are imposed over the heads of local authorities. The Archbishop of Canterbury's Commission
on Urban Priority Areas noted that the city authorities 'have lost far more in Rate Support Grant than
they have gained under the Urban Programme . . .
There is one exception: the only main central
government expenditure programme to have shown

43

a significant growth in the inner cities in real terms since 1979 is that on the police.'

If anyone needs convincing, an authoritative report by the Town and Country Planning Association provides examples: 'Manchester City Council gained in real terms an extra £9 million via the Urban Programme between 1980–81 and 1984–85, while losing some £100 million in Rate Support Grant settlements within the same period.' In London in the period 1979–80 to 1983–84, 'Inner London gained £261 million in Urban Programme funding while losing £865 million in Rate Support Grant and a sizeable proportion of the £791 million of housing subsidy lost to London (1980–81 prices).'

We have already described the creeping centralisation of Britain. In the last decade the creep has become a gallop. We don't blame the government. We blame the British. We are glaringly out of step with other European countries in this. If you read the textbook history of Europe in the nineteenth century you will learn that the big events were seen as the Unification of Germany under Bismarck and Wilhelm I and the Unification of Italy under Cavour, Garibaldi, Mazzini and Victor Emmanuel I. Historians seldom pause to comment that these events were disasters for the people of Germany and Italy as well as for those of every other European nation.

But today, if you ask yourself which are the most decentralised countries in Europe, you will be obliged to conclude that, apart from the example of Switzerland, they are the Federal Republic of Germany and the Italian Republic. In Italy, local administration at city and regional level is strong and active. It is only those centrally administered services such as schooling and the post that Italians see as a disgrace. The Federal Republic of Germany is divided into *Länder* (states), *Landkreise* (counties) and *Gemeinden* (communes), each with revenue-gathering powers. The eleven *Länder* have considerable autonomy. The British have always smiled in superior fashion at the way France is centralised in Paris without noticing that Britain is now far more drastically centralised on London, while since 1983 France has completely reversed its centralist tradition and given real power to its twenty-two regional and its ninety-six departmental administrations as well as its 36,433 communes. Spain too is continually devolving.

But today it must be admitted that the most centralised state in Europe, with a few obvious exceptions such as Romania and Albania, is the United Kingdom.

This coincides, among our neighbours abroad, not only with actual measures of decentralisation but also with a growing concept of a 'Europe of the Regions', signifying that ancient regional entities are becoming more important than nation states. This is why it was a shrewd move on the part of the Scottish National Party to adopt the policy of 'Independence within Europe'. The prophet of this trend was Leopold Kohr, Austrian by birth and Welsh by adoption. In his remarkable book *The Breakdown of Nations* he advocates a small-state world, based on its genuine component parts rather than on the results of military force. 'Europe's problem,' he insists, 'is one of division, not union.'

But this is, to an extraordinary degree, Britain's problem. Belatedly, in 1989, the leader of the Labour Party assured the Party's Scottish conference that, 'We hold it to be self-evident that there must be established in the capital of Scotland a democratic, directly-elected assembly with relevant powers to be exercised in Scotland for the Scottish people.' He has not yet given such an undertaking for Wales.

The enormous advantage for the English of devolution in Scotland and Wales (we deliberately ignore the problem of Northern Ireland, imprisoned in the history of British imperialism) is that it would open the way for devolution in England. Roy Hattersley recognised this in advocating elected regional assemblies, only to be rebuked by John Garrett, Labour M P for Norwich, who warned that Mr Hattersley's plans to pass economic and political power to the regions would mean a Labour government 'handing over more than half the nation's population to the mercies of Tory-dominated regional governments in the East, South-east, South-west and probably the Midlands and London'. He said that the proposal was 'little more than an attempt at an electoral pact with the Tories: "You run your fiefdoms in the South while we run ours in the North"'. This comment implies that any party that gains a majority of Members of Parliament at Westminster is entitled to assume dictatorial powers over the entire country in pre-cisely the way that the present government has, or that any predecessor had. This is why Scotland, where the Labour Party has forty-eight members of Parliament out of seventy-two, is subject to every whim of a minority government hundreds of miles away.

The demand for regional autonomy is inevitable, and supporters of any party will choose to hasten or delay it. We have forecast that the last to yield will be the Treasury, the government department with supreme powers of revenue-gathering. The power of local authorities at every level to gather income without reference to central government has, as we have shown, been whittled down to an ever-decreasing proportion of local spending in the form of the domestic and business rate, essentially a tax on the occupation of property. It has few defenders, but nor has the poll tax or Community

Charge that is to supersede the domestic rate. We have no need to attack it, since it condemns itself for its regressive nature: it is nothing to the Duke of Westminster but it weighs heavily on his cleaner.

But with the introduction of the poll tax, councils are no longer able to set their own business rate. This will be pooled and redistributed in proportion to adult population. Brian Smith, County Treasurer of Staffordshire, warns that 'Central government will regard the business rate as part of the overall exchequer contribution to local government, and will as a consequence be tempted to regard itself as having direct control over about seventy-five per cent of local authority funding.'

Any advocate of decentralisation has to tackle the revenue aspect. What is the point of regional administration if it depends on the policies of a central Chancellor of the Exchequer? We can fantasise in several ways about alternative proposals. Suppose the British had decided on a policy of Switzerisation and broke down the Inland Revenue into branches of regional government, grudgingly paying over a proportion to Whitehall for federal purposes? Or if that is going too far for your taste, suppose that regional and local councils were to levy a local income tax simply by a precept on the Inland Revenue in the same way that county councils have a precept on district council rates today? In Swiss cantons the obvious difficulty that many people live in one district and work in another is overcome by a proportional split of local taxes.

Beyond our plea for creative accountancy in the form of fiscal imagination in a decentralised Britain, the question arises of the size and nature of local democracy. Most authorities on local government would agree that the re-organisation of London government in 1964 and of that of the rest of England and Wales in 1974 was an expensive disaster. The one thing the country cannot face is a further re-organisation. There is good reason for this. We spend half a lifetime coming to terms with the locality we feel part of. If some administrative decision re-defines it, we may feel lost for the rest of our lives.

Edmund Burke expressed this well two hundred years ago, speaking of 'our neighbourhoods and our habitual provincial connections'. These, he claimed, 'are inns and resting places, such divisions of our country as have been formed by habit, and not by a sudden jerk of authority'. Imagine yourself born in the North Riding of Yorkshire and identifying yourself with that county, only to find in adult life that you had joined the County Borough of Middlesborough. Having tried to shake down with this new identity, you found yourself transformed in 1968 into the County Borough of Teesside, along with the citizens of Stockton-on-Tees, Redcar, Billingham, Thornaby and Eston. Re-designating yourself as a Teessider, you had to make yet another re-adjustment only six years later when learning that you actually belonged to Cleveland, an entity you had not heard of, except as the address of relatives in Ohio.

It was once thought a virtue for children to grow up knowing where places were. We had jigsaw puzzles to teach us painlessly the locations of British towns and counties. How many of our readers can instantly locate and differentiate between Tameside, Thamesdown and Thamesmead, names which all conceal recognisable places?

The first essential of popular public administration is not uniformity but comprehensibility. And when the British gradually decide to reverse the twentieth-century drift into centralisation, we may expect an untidy pattern full of anomalies and absurdities like those of Switzerland. The county of Rutland may re-emerge and decide to issue its own postage stamps. Who will worry except that minority of bureaucrats who identify with central government's civil service, its mandarin hierarchy and its contempt for the local?

Just as the whole tendency in the twentieth century has been an unthinking assumption that central government knows best, so the inevitable reaction in the twenty-first century is going to be a rediscovery of the aspirations towards local democracy. There is going to be a devolution of control of essentially community concerns from district and county councils to local communities. There is going to be a devolution of control of essentially regional concerns from central government to regional bodies as federations of counties.

We are certain that the scale and scope of self-government will become the major political and social issue of the next century. This will be because our own century has been littered by the disasters and follies of dictators and democrats who dismissed local autonomy as unimportant or as an obstacle to their own grand ambitions. In 1835 Alexis de Tocqueville summed up his study of democracy: 'The strength of free peoples,' he found, 'resides in the local community. Local institutions are to liberty what primary schools are to science; they put it within the people's reach; they teach people to appreciate its peaceful enjoyment and accustom them to make use of it. Without local institutions a nation may give itself a free government but it has not got the spirit of liberty.'

He went on to explain that, 'I do not think one could find a single inhabitant of New England who would recognise the right of the government of the state to control matters of purely municipal interest.' The municipalities he was describing were no bigger than the parishes of Kersey or Polstead. Maybe when we revisit them in 2051 we shall find that the same comment can be made of England too.

No political party was ever elected to office with a mandate to prevent primary school children from attending school in their own village, nor young adults from housing themselves in the same community as their parents. No political philosophy, right, left or centre, has the elimination of locality as an article of belief. It just happens. The task of citizens of all political persuasions, and of none, is consequently to undermine the central line.

References

The Breakdown of Nations by Leopold Kohr, Routledge
& Kegan Paul, 1957

Captain Swing by E. J. Hobsbawm and George Rude,
Penguin, 1973

A Century of Scottish People 1830–1950 by T. C. Smout,
Collins, 1986

Children and their Primary Schools (The Plowden Report),
HMSO, 1967

Democracy in America by Alexis de Tocqueville, Fontana,
1968

Enlisting the Community to Fight Rural Problems, District
Councils Review, January 1989

Faith in the City: a Call for Action by Church and Nation,
Church House Publishing, 1985

Government by Community by Ioan Bowen Rees, Charles
Knight & Co, 1971

'Has Switzerland a Future?', *Encounter*, December 1962

Local Government Chronicle, article by Ivor Gowan, 2
May 1970

Local Government in Britain by Tony Byrne, Pelican,
1987

'Memorandum of Dissent' by D. Senior, *Report of the
Royal Commission on Local Government in England
1966–69, Vol II*, HMSO, 1969

News from Nowhere by William Morris, Penguin, 1986

The Politics of Local Socialism by John Gyford, Allen & Unwin, 1985

Polstead School, Appeal to the Secretary of State by Bensusan, Blackham and others, 1988

A Property-Owning Democracy: Housing in Britain by M. J. Daunton, Faber & Faber, 1987

Speeches, Vol I by Joseph Chamberlain, ed. by C. W. Boyd, Constable, 1914

The Surveyor, January 28, 1988

Whose Responsibility? Reclaiming the Inner Cities, Town and Country Planning Association, TCPA, 1986

Why Switzerland? by Jonathan Steinberg, Cambridge University Press, 1976

Writings and Speeches, Vol II by Edmund Burke, Clarendon Press, 1981

About the Authors

RUTH RENDELL has been writing fiction since 1964 and three of her novels – *A Demon in My View*, *Live Flesh*, and *A Fatal Inversion* – have been awarded the Crime Writer's Association Gold Dagger for best crime novel. Her novel *Lake of Darkness* won the Arts Council Genre Fiction award in 1980 and *The Tree of Hands* won a Silver Dagger in 1985. Ruth Rendell also writes under the pseudonym of Barbara Vine and her books have been translated into seventeen languages.

COLIN WARD was given the first Charles Douglas-Home Memorial Trust Award to write his most recent book, *Welcome, Thinner City*. His other books include *The Child in the Country* and (with David Crouch) *The Allotment: its landscape and culture*. His book *Anarchy in Action* has been translated into seven languages, including Hungarian and Japanese.

CHATTO
Counter*Blasts*

Also available in bookshops now:-

Counter*Blasts* to be published in 1990 include:-

Christopher Hitchens on the Monarchy
Tessa Blackstone on prisons and penal reform
Douglas Dunn on Poll Tax
Ludovic Kennedy on Euthanasia
Adam Mars-Jones on Venus Envy
Adam Lively on sovereignty
Margaret Drabble on property and mortgage tax relief
Ronald Dworkin on a Bill of Rights for Britain

plus pamphlets from Michael Holroyd, Harold Evans, Hanif
Kureishi, Michael Ignatieff, Edward Mortimer and Susannah
Clapp

If you want to join in the debate, and if you want to know more
about **Counter*Blasts***, the writers and the issues, then write to:

Random House UK Ltd, Freepost 5066, Dept MH, London
WC1B 3BR